12 Days of Christmas in Stickleback Hollow

The Mysteries of Stickleback Hollow

By C.S. Woolley

A Mightier Than the Sword UK Publication

©2017

12 Days of Christmas in Stickleback Hollow

The Mysteries of Stickleback Hollow

By C. S. Woolley

A Mightier Than the Sword UK Publication

Paperback Edition

Paperback ISBN 978-0-9951471-5-7

Hardback ISBN 978-0-9951471-6-4

ePub ISBN 978-0-9951471-7-1

Kindle ISBN 978-0-9951471-8-8

iBook ISBN 975-0-9951471-9-5

For

The Broad Appeal and the Trent Bridge Community Sports Trust

Author's Note

Thanks for taking the time to read *12 Days of Christmas in Stickleback Hollow*; I hope you enjoy it, as well as the other books in the series. This book is in aid of the Broad Appeal and the Trent Bridge Community Sports Trust.

The Broad Appeal raises money for MNDA and further details about the charity can be found at http://thebroadappeal.org.

The Trent Bridge Community Sports Trust is a charity that is the charitable arm of Nottinghamshire County Cricket Club which aims to give a sporting chance to the disadvantaged young people in Nottinghamshire. You can find out more details here: http://www.trentbridge.co.uk/trust.

As far as where these stories fit in the narrative, they take place at different Christmas ranging from Mr Hunter's childhood to Lady Sarah's tenure at the manor.

I hope they give you a good measure of the season and though for many it can be filled with joy and happiness, not every Christmas is so.

The 12 Days of Christmas

On the first day of Christmas

my true love gave to me:

A Partridge in a Pear Tree

On the second day of Christmas

my true love gave to me:

Two Turtle Doves

and a Partridge in a Pear Tree

On the third day of Christmas

my true love gave to me:

Three French Hens

Two Turtle Doves

and a Partridge in a Pear Tree

On the fourth day of Christmas

my true love gave to me:

Four Calling Birds

Three French Hens

Two Turtle Doves

and a Partridge in a Pear Tree

On the fifth day of Christmas

my true love gave to me:

Five Golden Rings

Four Calling Birds

Three French Hens

Two Turtle Doves

and a Partridge in a Pear Tree

On the sixth day of Christmas

my true love gave to me:

Six Geese a Laying

Five Golden Rings

Four Calling Birds

Three French Hens

Two Turtle Doves

and a Partridge in a Pear Tree

On the seventh day of Christmas

my true love gave to me:

Seven Swans a Swimming

Six Geese a Laying

Five Golden Rings

Four Calling Birds

Three French Hens

Two Turtle Doves

and a Partridge in a Pear Tree

On the eighth day of Christmas

my true love gave to me:

Eight Maids a Milking

Seven Swans a Swimming

Six Geese a Laying

Five Golden Rings

Four Calling Birds

Three French Hens

Two Turtle Doves

and a Partridge in a Pear Tree

On the ninth day of Christmas

my true love gave to me:

Nine Ladies Dancing

Eight Maids a Milking

Seven Swans a Swimming

Six Geese a Laying

Five Golden Rings

Four Calling Birds

Three French Hens

Two Turtle Doves

and a Partridge in a Pear Tree

On the tenth day of Christmas

my true love gave to me:

Ten Drummers Drumming

Nine Ladies Dancing

Eight Maids a Milking

Seven Swans a Swimming

Six Geese a Laying

Five Golden Rings

Four Calling Birds

Three French Hens

Two Turtle Doves

and a Partridge in a Pear Tree

On the eleventh day of Christmas

my true love gave to me:

Eleven Pipers Piping

Ten Drummers Drumming

Nine Ladies Dancing

Eight Maids a Milking

Seven Swans a Swimming

Six Geese a Laying

Five Golden Rings

Four Calling Birds

Three French Hens

Two Turtle Doves

and a Partridge in a Pear Tree

On the twelfth day of Christmas

my true love gave to me:

Twelve Lords a Leaping

Eleven Pipers Piping

Ten Drummers Drumming

Nine Ladies Dancing

Eight Maids a Milking

Seven Swans a Swimming

Six Geese a Laying

Five Golden Rings

Four Calling Birds

Three French Hens

Two Turtle Doves

and a Partridge in a Pear Tree

1ˢᵗ Day of Christmas

On the first day of Christmas, my true love gave to me, a Partridge in a Pear Tree

Mr Alexander Hunter crept silently through the woods that bordered the Grangeback Estate and the village of Stickleback Hollow. There was snow covering the ground, and the lake that lay beyond the trees had frozen a few weeks ago. There was a fishing boat that was stuck in the ice, which showed no signs of thawing. Lee and Stanley Baker had gone out fishing during the night and fallen asleep in the boat. When the sun had risen, the two boys had screamed when they discovered that they were stranded in the ice.

Alex had heard the two boys and wandered into Stickleback to fetch their mother, Miss Baker, and Constable Arwen Evans. Constable Evans and Mr Hunter had walked out onto the ice and carried the boys back to the shore, where Miss Baker dragged the boys home by their ears, giving them the greatest tongue lashing of their life.

The two boys hadn't been back to the woods or the lake since then. During the winter months, the people of Stickleback Hollow didn't venture into the forest, except on Christmas morning. There was a tradition in the village that called for everyone to wake up early on Christmas morning and walk through the trees on their way to the chapel that lay in the grounds of the Grangeback Estate. There was a church in the village, but the Christmas service was held in the chapel, and then everyone was invited to eat Christmas dinner at the manor.

This tradition went back 400 years, to when the Kneelingroach family had first taken possession of the estate. Before the brigadier retired from the army and returned to England from India, it had been in the hands of his older brother, who had also upheld the tradition.

It was one of Alex's favourite parts of Christmas, especially as he was responsible for bringing the gift to the house this year. Every year, the village gave a gift to the manor as a thank you for Christmas dinner. The table was always full of food that included geese that were reared on the estate, especially for the Yuletide dinner. The gift was always something that the household could use, something that was useful, rather than simply decorative. Miss Baker had made gloves, hats and scarves for all the members of the household the year before as the gift from the village, and the year before that, the blacksmith, Mr James Fletcher, had presented Brigadier Webb-Kneelingroach with new horseshoes for all the horses on the estate.

However, this year, Alex wanted to do something different. He was stalking through the trees an hour before the village of Stickleback Hollow would be stirring in search of the perfect present to take. He checked the traps that he had set in the forest and found that all but one was empty. But the trap that was full, that had exactly what he needed in it.

He stole back to the lodge that he lived in to prepare the gift and then took it up to the house and placed it in the corner of the dining room under a heavy cloth so that no one would see it until the Christmas dinner began. Grangeback was full of the smell of food already. Cooky had been up all night preparing the feast for the next day. It was ready and placed in the serving dishes before she left for church so that it stayed hot. The dining room was set the night before by Bosworth and Mrs Bosworth. The table was covered with fine china, silver, crystal goblets, decanters of wine and space down the centre of the table for the serving dishes. The fireplace had a fire built in it that was ready to light when they came back from church.

Everything was ready, so Alex walked down to the village to be part of the procession to the church. The sound of snow crunching underfoot was a welcome sound in the woods; it made them seem almost alive as the people of Stickleback Hollow filed into the chapel. The brigadier greeted everyone at the door, and the Reverend Percy Butterfield held the service.

The hymns were sung, the lesson was read, and the story of the birth of Jesus Christ was told. It was the same service that was held every year, and once it was over, the people of Stickleback Hollow filed out of the chapel and walked towards Grangeback.

The fire was lit in the dining room, the wine was poured, the food was brought to the table, and the happy sound of friends enjoying Christmas together echoed throughout the corridors of the Manor house. Once the pudding had been eaten, the table cleared and all the plates washed, everyone waited with bated breath to see what the gift to the household would be.

Alex stood and walked to the corner of the room. He stood next to the cloth that covered the gift and took a deep breath. In a single, smooth motion, he pulled the cloth to the side to reveal a large gilded cage that had inside it a tree with a bird sat asleep on one of the branches.

"My dear boy, what is it?" the brigadier asked.

"George, this year the village of Stickleback Hollow is honoured to present you and the household of Grangeback with a partridge in a pear tree," Alex smiled.

2nd Day of Christmas

On the 2nd day of Christmas, my true love gave to me, two turtle doves.

George Webb-Kneelingroach looked out at the lands of his family estate. His family had spent generations on this land, back before the house of Grangeback had been designed and built. The family crypt was in the grounds of the chapel and held the Kneelingroach line as well as that of the Webbs.

He was sat in the rooms that had once belonged to his daughter, Lucy. She had been a bright girl, enjoyed her life in England and India in equal measure, and Christmas had always been her favourite time of year. She would roam the halls of Grangeback singing Christmas Carols until the whole household couldn't stop singing them. It brought a great deal of joy to the manor and to Stickleback Hollow. There was hardly a person, from the Grangeback groundskeeper to the village lamplighter, that wasn't infected with a cheerful demeanour after Lucy had visited the village around Christmas.

She not only believed in sharing good cheer but making sure that everyone in the village had all they needed. When the blacksmith burnt his hand and couldn't use his forge, Lucy sent to Chester for an apprentice to work for him. When the vicar had a fever, Lucy nursed him back to health. There was nothing that was too much trouble for her.

George sat and looked at his beloved Grangeback and thought about the last Christmas that Lucy had spent there. She had been visiting the village three weeks before Christmas when she met a young man from London. He was a well-dressed individual that had no business being in Stickleback Hollow, at least as far as George could see. He was staying at the inn and told everyone that he was there to enjoy walking the countryside.

After Lucy met him, he started to join her walking around the village every day and after two weeks; he invited her to the theatre. It was a performance in Manchester and Lucy went without an escort in her finest clothes. George didn't know what it was that they saw at the theatre; all he knew was that Lucy didn't come home that night. It was two days before she returned to the house and declared that she was engaged. The young man hadn't been to Grangeback or asked for George's permission to marry his daughter before he had propositioned Lucy.

George had insisted that Lucy bring him to the house to meet the family before anything else was said on the subject of her engagement. The next day Lucy had gone down to the village, only to find the young man was gone. The innkeeper said that he had left the night before and had no intention of returning. Lucy returned to the house and burst into floods of tears.

She was taken ill and even missed the village's traditional Christmas dinner. She was in bed for a month, and George grew very concerned and sent for the doctor. The doctor had come to visit and gave George the grave news – Lucy was pregnant. It was then that the young man's intention had become clear and George sent for his solicitor. A search was made of each of the cities under the name that Lucy had been given, but the young man couldn't be found.

The doctor suggested that Lucy and the family go to Scotland until the baby had been born and return to Stickleback Hollow with the babe in arms, a sibling to Lucy rather than her child. George agreed and had his wife, Helen and her lady's maid, Emma, pack for the months that they would be absent for the manor. Bosworth was left in charge of Grangeback in their absence and was sworn to secrecy about the whole matter.

The journey to Scotland had begun in the New Year and had not been a comfortable one. The family estate in Scotland belonged to Helen Webb-Kneelingroach and was in the far-flung highlands where the only people for miles were those who served the household, and their families had done so for several centuries.

Lucy understood the importance of the child

being raised as her sibling and not as her child and seemed to be content enough with the arrangement that her father and the doctor had agreed upon. For months they enjoyed walking across the highlands. Her mother was happy to be at the place she had called home and even happier that a new life should enter the world there.

But it was not to be. Before her nine months were up, Lucy woke in the night, screaming in pain. There was nothing that could be done to ease her distress or that of the baby. The women of the household did all that they could, the doctor in Stickleback Hollow was sent for, he arrived to find that Lucy had gone into labour two months before she should have. He worked tirelessly to save the mother and child, but he had arrived too late.

Helen shut herself in her rooms and refused to allow anyone in, not even her lady's maid. The doctor made arrangements to have Lucy and the baby taken back to Stickleback where they could be buried in the family crypt, and George had been left to his misery.

There had been no Christmas Carols sung in the halls of Grangeback since that day.

George sighed as he looked out of the windows and wondered what it was that drove young men to callously throw aside the virtue of young women when he heard the sound of singing coming from the music room.

"Adeste Fideles laeti triumphantes,
Venite, venite in Bethlehem.
Natum videte, Regem Angelorum;

    Venite adoremus,
    venite adoremus,
    venite adoremus
    Dominum!

Deum de Deo, lumen de lumine,
gestant puellae viscera.
Deum verum, genitum non factum;

Venite adoremus,

venite adoremus,

venite adoremus

Dominum!

Cantet nunc io chorus Angelorum

cantet nunc aula caelestium:

Gloria in excelsis Deo!

Venite adoremus,

venite adoremus,

venite adoremus

Dominum!

Ergo qui natus, die hodierna,

Jesu, tibi sit gloria.

Patris aeterni Verbum caro factum;

Venite adoremus,

venite adoremus,

venite adoremus

Dominum!

En grege relicto, Humiles ad cunas,

vocati pastores approperant.

Et nos ovanti gradu festinemus;

Venite adoremus,

venite adoremus,

venite adoremus

Dominum!

Aeterni Parentis splendorem aeternum,

velatum sub carne videbimus.

Deum infantem, pannis involutum;

Venite adoremus,

venite adoremus,

venite adoremus

Dominum!

Pro nobis egenum et foeno cubantem,

piis foveamus amplexibus.

Sic nos anamtem quis non redamaret?

Venite adoremus,

venite adoremus,

venite adoremus

Dominum!

Stella duce, Magi, Christum adorantes,

aurum, thus, et myrrham dant munera."

It was Sarah; she was playing the piano and singing to herself. George rushed down the hall to find Alex was the one playing the piano whilst Sarah sang. Mrs Bosworth, Bosworth, Cooky, the maids and other servants were all gathered around the doorway listening to the two of them perform. The pair were quite unaware that they had an audience.

"Oh brigadier, it's been so long since there was music in the house. Doesn't it feel like Christmas now?"

Cooky whispered as she saw George approaching.

"Yes, Cooky, it certainly does," George replied.

3rd Day of Christmas

On the third day of Christmas, my true love gave to me, three French hens.

There was a lot of work to do in the Manor of Grangeback. The maids were all busy cleaning the dining room after the village had all been to Christmas dinner. It took a week of cleaning to set the house to rights after Christmas Day. This was mostly because of the mess that several hundred people all getting together in one place created, but also down to the hours that the maids worked during the 12 days of Christmas.

The 2nd day of Christmas was also Boxing Day and a day when all the servants in the house were given the day to spend with their families and visiting friends, not working. The brigadier was left to his own devices on Boxing Day, which often led to more mess being created in a single day than the village could create in a week visiting the house. Not all the household staff would spend Boxing Day away from the manor, but no one would do any work.

Then on the 3rd day, there was the cleaning and tidying to begin. Mrs Bosworth would oversee the cleaning, whilst Bosworth attended to the brigadier, mostly so he couldn't create any more chaos than he already had. The maids, the footmen, the housemen and the hall boys were all called away from their normal duties in order to set the house to rights; all except for Cooky.

Cooky never had to help with the cleaning on the 3rd day of Christmas as she was busy ensuring that the pantry was restocked from the village, cooking enough food to keep the household staff from going hungry as they worked and planning the meals for visitors the house was expecting during the other nine days of Christmas.

The kitchens were the one room in the house that didn't need cleaning on the 3rd day of Christmas. The people of Stickleback Hollow were very good at helping to tidy away the kitchen, and the brigadier spent the 2nd day of Christmas eating what was left over from the grand Christmas dinner. For Cooky, the 3rd day of Christmas was almost relaxing. She spent the morning talking to the people of Stickleback Hollow as she ordered food for the house and had it loaded into one of the carts for the manor. After she had prepared lunch for the house, she walked out into the herb garden that was housed in a glass hothouse, stopping the cold winter snow from killing off the more exotic plants that had been brought to the house over the years.

Once she had gathered the herbs she needed, she went to check on the hens. There were thirteen of them in total, four of them were Sussex hens, three of them were Dorking hens, two were Malay hens, and four were Cornish hens. Cooky had chosen all the birds herself and was always looking to add more to her own little hen house. The eggs she gathered from these hens were used for special dishes, rather than the eggs that she bought from the village that were used in most of her cooking.

Cooky waddled up to the chicken coop and found that there was something different about her hens.

Instead of thirteen of them, there were sixteen. There were three interlopers. One was white, one was black, and the other was grey. Cooky stood there in shock for a moment as she tried to work out what breed the hens were.

"They're Gauloise," Mr Hunter said from outside of the chicken coop. Cooky jumped in surprise and caused the hens closest to her to flutter away in a fuss.

"Mr Hunter! Oh, my. What a fright you gave me. How do you know they are Gauloise?" Cooky asked as she patted her chest over her heart.

"Because I was there when Lady Sarah bought them," Alex smiled.

"Lady Sarah bought them?" Cooky asked as she eyed the birds.

"Yes, she wanted to do something to say thank you to you for all the hard work you put into her first Christmas dinner here," Mr Hunter replied.

"How did she know to get me hens?" Cooky frowned as she started to move around the birds to collect the eggs from the nests.

"She asked Mrs Bosworth what you wanted, and then asked me to take her to find something suitable," Alex said as he watched Cooky bustling about.

"Well, they are wonderful; I will have to tell her how nice they are when I see her," Cooky instructed herself, "wait; if they are a thank you for the Christmas dinner, that was two days ago, when did you go get them?"

"At dawn this morning."

"Of all the soft things to do," Cooky sighed.

"Well, I'm glad you like them, Cooky. Now, if you'll excuse me, I have some pheasants to shoot and some hares to snare," Alex said and waved to Cooky as he went to stalk through the long grass of the estate.

Cooky clucked around her hen house for a few hours, she was enjoying spending time with her new hens, so much so that she lost track of time.

"Cooky! What are you doing out here?" Mrs Bosworth cried as she came striding out to the chicken coop.

"I'm getting to know my new birds, what's

wrong, Mrs Bosworth?" Cooky asked.

"The brigadier is moaning about his afternoon tea being late, and there are no scones to send out with it!" Mrs Bosworth huffed.

"Oh! I forgot all about the scones, and it's going to be dark soon. Oh dear, how behind I am!" Cooky clucked as she made her way out of the hen house and back to the manor. Mrs Bosworth stood in the snow and shook her head as she watched Cooky go.

"That woman and her hens," Mrs Bosworth sighed and shuffled back to the house to check on the progress of the maids.

4ᵗʰ Day of Christmas

On the fourth day of Christmas, my true love gave to me, four colly birds.

Doctor Jack Hales sat in his house, sipping on a glass of sherry in front of a large fire. The doctor had done well in his life. He lived in a village that was an interesting place to live and was much more pleasant than any city he had ever visited.

He had spent the day visiting the Manchester Royal Infirmary to help the doctors with an influx of people suffering from chest infections. There had been so many this year that the doctors had been struggling to cope before Jack had arrived.

"Father, you're back," his son, Richard said as he walked into the library where the doctor sat.

"Yes, it didn't take as long as I thought it would," the doctor yawned and took another sip from his glass.

"Well, that's very nice, but we weren't expecting

you back until tomorrow," Richard said, looking furtive.

"What are you up to?" the doctor frowned at his oldest son.

"Nothing," Richard said, trying to sound off-hand.

"Where is your brother?" the doctor asked as he put down his sherry and leaned forward on his knees.

"Nowhere," Richard replied too quickly.

"You always were a terrible liar," the doctor tutted.

"Please, don't ruin things, father. Promise me you won't ask any questions and that you will stay here until we come and get you," Richard begged.

"Fine, but if whatever the two of you are up to gets Constable Evans coming to visit us again, your lives won't be worth living," the doctor warned.

Richard disappeared from the room quickly, and the doctor picked up his sherry again. He loved his sons dearly. He had raised them alone as his wife had died giving birth to his youngest son, Gordon. Richard was almost thirty in age and was training to be a doctor. He had tried a few different career paths before deciding to follow in his father's footsteps. Gordon was in his mid-twenties and training to be a lawyer. Both boys had applied themselves to their studies, and the doctor was proud of them, though he rarely expressed such emotion.

The two boys, though studious, also had a knack for getting into trouble. They often argued over the same girls, and though neither seemed inclined to marry, they were in and out of love as often as the moon changed.

In the next room, the doctor could hear shuffling and the odd expletive being uttered as his two sons worked on whatever surprise it was that they had in store. The doctor had an uneasy feeling about it all, but he was a man of his word, so he waited patiently until Gordon and Richard came to fetch him.

The two boys were grinning as they led their father into the next room where there was a coup of four blackbirds sat by the windows.

"What is this?" the doctor asked.

"Well, you said that you always wanted birds to send messages with to the hospital to save on sending messengers from the village. So we went into Chester and found these," Gordon smiled.

"We thought they'd be less likely to be shot at than pigeons. Not many people like colly bird pie around here," Richard grinned.

5th Day of Christmas

On the fifth day of Christmas, my true love gave to me, five gold rings.

The sun was bright in the sky as Sarah awoke on Christmas morning. She could hear the sounds of the household bustling through the white marble corridors. She rolled over and closed her eyes. She waited until she heard the door to the room open and her ayah walk in.

"Still abed on Christmas morning?" ayah asked as she pulled back the sheets and Sarah buried her head under the pillow.

"It's too early," Sarah's moan was muffled by the pillow.

"When you and your mother were little girls, both of you used to jump out of bed before most of the household had woken up to see if there were any gifts for you," ayah said shaking her head and pulling the pillows off the bed.

"I'm not a little girl anymore, ayah," Sarah whined and tried to grab the pillow back from her nanny.

"No, now you're a young lady and should start acting like it. At your age, your mother was married to your father. Nearly all girls your age are married and expecting families," ayah clucked as she disappeared into Sarah's dressing room to get out her clothes for the day.

Sarah sighed and sprawled out on her bed before she rolled out of her bed and traipsed over to her dressing room. Ayah had taken out a white muslin dress and a long white lace shawl that was pinned over her shoulder. Sarah stood with her arms out as ayah washed and dressed her.

"You'll do," ayah said finally, and Sarah left her room to go enjoy breakfast.

Her mother and father were both sat out on the veranda, enjoying their breakfast whilst looking out at the Indian countryside that lay around their home.

"Merry Christmas," Sarah said as she walked out onto the patio.

"Merry Christmas, my love," Colonel

Montgomery Baird said without looking up from the book he was reading.

"Merry Christmas, there are some visitors waiting to see you," Lady Watson-Wentworth said and led Sarah away from the breakfast. Sarah glanced at the breakfast table with longing as she was led back into the house to a sitting room where five young men were waiting.

Each of them were dressed in the uniforms of lieutenants, and all seemed to be very nervous. Sarah looked at her mother with a raised eyebrow as she saw the five lieutenants.

"Gentlemen, please place the rings on the table on your calling card and then address my daughter as my lady. When she is finished talking to you, you will be escorted out by the butler. An answer will be returned with your calling card. If she rejects your proposal, then the ring will also be returned with your card," Lady Cynthia Watson-Wentworth said in a clear voice.

"Mother," Sarah said in protest as her mother turned to leave the room.

"Good luck, dear," Lady Cynthia said as she

patted her daughter's arm and kissed her cheek.

Sarah turned back to face the five lieutenants and looked down at the five gold rings that lay on the table on the velvet pillow that had the five calling cards on.

"This is not what I wanted for Christmas," she said under her breath as the first lieutenant approached her.

6th Day of Christmas

On the sixth day of Christmas, my true love gave to me, six geese a laying.

Mrs Bosworth was not a woman that liked to do very much, aside from work. She hated to sit down and waste time; after all, there was always something better that she could be doing, especially around Christmas. Mr and Mrs Bosworth had no children of their own, three had been born, and all died before they had reached the age of five.

For Mrs Bosworth, it made Christmas a rather difficult time of year. Mr Bosworth had borne the loss of two sons and a daughter with remarkable fortitude and had buried himself in his duties at Grangeback. Mrs Bosworth had looked on Lucy Kneelingroach as a surrogate daughter, satisfying her maternal instincts by mothering the young lady. When she had died, it had caused Mrs Bosworth to become even more fastidious than she had been before.

Every Boxing Day, when she and Mr Bosworth were not working, Mrs Bosworth would sink into a quiet depression. She didn't speak a word to Mr Bosworth for the whole day, but sat in their room, holding an armful of old knitted geese. When Mrs Bosworth was pregnant, she spent her evenings knitting things for the baby she was expecting. She wasn't very adept at knitting but had skill enough to create blankets and toy geese. Each pregnancy she had done the same thing – knitted two blankets and two geese. The blankets had been put to good use when Lucy had been a baby, but Mrs Bosworth couldn't bring herself to give the geese to the young lady of the house. Instead, she kept them for herself, a reminder of the children she had once had and the short time she had to cradle them before they were taken from her.

Mr Bosworth never tried to take the geese from his wife, nor did he offer any word of comfort. He knew that there was nothing that he could say that would make the loss of their children any better. When their daughter had died, Mrs Bosworth had told her husband that she couldn't take losing another child and the two had agreed that there would be no more children. Mr Bosworth was a man that kept his feelings to himself, he had his own pain over the loss of his children, but he didn't want to burden his wife when he knew of the pain she was suffering. He consoled himself every year by watching his wife as she cuddled the six geese and gazed out of the window at the lake.

7th Day of Christmas

On the seventh day of Christmas, my true love gave to me, seven swans a swimming.

"Are you ready?" Lee asked his brother. The two of them had waited until their mother had gone out to her shop for the day before they made their plans. The two boys had been adopted by Miss Baker when they had been found on the doorstep of her seamstress shop.

"Are you sure this is a good idea?" Stanley asked as he followed Lee out of the small house that stood on the edge of the village of Stickleback Hollow.

"Of course! We need to go get our boat back," Lee smiled at him. Both of the boys knew that Miss Baker wasn't their real mother, but their family was closer than most that were related by blood. Stanley worked as the boy for the butcher, and Lee was the boy for the baker. Both boys started working long before their mother rose to go to her shop, but the boys always came back for breakfast before she left.

Christmas was always a quiet and enjoyable affair for the family. They spent Christmas Day at Grangeback and then on Boxing Day they went for a walk around the woods. It had been on Boxing Day that Lee had begun to plan rescuing their boat from the frozen lake. Stanley hadn't wanted to go back to the lake ever again, but his brother was far more convincing than Stanley liked.

It had taken three days for Lee to talk his brother into his scheme and a day to gather the items that they would need in order to get their boat back. Lee had borrowed some pikes from the blacksmith without the old man knowing; promising Stanley that he would return them once the boat was safely back ashore.

The two boys set out from the house and went around the edge of the village, making sure that no one saw them as they went. They ran as quickly as they could until they reached the safety of the tree line. The two boys paused in the trees to catch their breath before they walked to the edge of the lake.

The snow was still thick on the ground, and the lake was frozen solid. The two boys walked gingerly across the ice until they reached their boat and climbed over the side of it. When they were both settled in the bottom of the boat, Lee handed Stanley one of the iron pikes he had stolen from the blacksmith. The two boys hit the ice around the boat until the boat was freed from the ice. Stanley took up the oars and started to manoeuvre the boat back towards the shore. Lee leaned over the side of the boat and kept breaking the ice in front of the boat until they reached the bank.

It was hard and slow work, but by the time they had finished, both of the boys felt proud of what they had accomplished.

"You know that if your mother finds out about this, you'll not be able to sit down for a week," Alex said. The two boys froze in the boat as they looked up at the hunter who stood on the shore, leaning against one of the trees.

"You're not going to tell her, are you?" Stanley asked as Lee jumped out of the boat and started to pull it onto the bank. Stanley followed his brother to help him get the boat out of the water.

"I won't need to; did you even think about what you are going to tell her when she sees that the boat isn't stuck in the lake anymore?" Alex asked with amusement.

"No," Lee said slowly.

"You told me that you'd thought of everything!" Stanley cried.

"I wouldn't worry about it too much," Alex smiled at the two boys.

"Why not?" Lee frowned.

"Leave the boat here, and I'll tell her I got it out for you," Alex said with a shrug.

"Why would you do that?" Stanley asked.

"Because you're going to need to put those pikes back before the blacksmith notices they are missing and because you haven't noticed what breaking the ice did for the lake," Alex grinned.

"What are you talking about?" Lee asked.

"Just look at the water," Alex said. Lee and Stanley both turned around and looked out at the lake. A group of seven swans had come out of the forest and was moving across the ice to the open water. The two boys watched as the swans slipped into the cold water and started swimming around.

8th Day of Christmas

On the eighth day of Christmas, my true love gave to me, eight maids a milking.

Christmas was always a busy time to be an innkeeper. Lots of people came to Stickleback Hollow to visit relatives in the nearby city of Chester and also in the village itself. Some people chose to stay in the inn that Wilson ran because his wife's cooking was known far and wide as the best in the area. Some people didn't like staying in the city as it was too busy and full of bustle.

Whatever the reasons that people came to the inn, Wilson and Emma were both very busy. Unlike the staff at the house and many others in the village, they didn't close, not even on Christmas Day. They went to the house for Christmas dinner after going to church, but they were always the first to leave as they had to get back to the inn. They made sure that all their guests knew that the doors of the inn would be locked from when they went to church until after Christmas dinner had finished, but this never seemed to be a problem as all their guests had prior plans for Christmas Day.

But on Boxing Day things were back to normal. In fact, the inn was often busier on Boxing Day than any other day of the year as people like the blacksmith and Miss Baker were not at work, and so came to the inn to talk and swap seasonal greetings – though they had all seen each other the day before.

Wilson liked running the inn, especially around Christmas. He didn't really need time off to put his feet up. There was nothing to do when he stopped working and often found the days when the inn had to be closed to be rather boring. Emma preferred to be busy, and even when the kitchen wasn't open, she could be seen bustling around the inn, making sure that everything was running smoothly.

One of the problems that faced the inn during the busy time of Christmas was the risk of running out of milk. Every day during Christmas, Wilson woke up early to walk out to one of the local dairy farms to get the farmer to buy more milk. When he walked down the path to the dairy farmer's house, he could hear the milkmaids singing in the small field that lay next to the house. The milkmaids were the daughters of farmers in the local area, but not all of them were the daughters of the dairy farmer. There were eight of them in all, and all of them enjoyed singing, though not one of them could carry a tune.

Wilson waved to them as he passed and went about his business with the farmer.

"It's a sad thing, but today is the last day you'll see those milkmaids," the farmer said as the two men walked outside to fetch the pails of milk for the inn.

"Why is that?" Wilson asked.

"They're all to be married, can't stay milkmaids forever. There are a bunch of young farmers coming later on today to meet them, then the dates for the weddings will be set, and the girls will be gone," the farmer sighed.

"Who is going to milk your cows?" Wilson asked.

"Oh, there are more girls coming to do that, the cows won't mind at all, but you might want to say your goodbyes. My two are going to be going down to Kent, only God knows where the others will end up," the farmer shrugged.

"Will they be well provided for?" Wilson asked.

"They will. I know all the boys that are coming to meet the girls, some haven't bought holdings yet, others will be going back to their father's farms. I'll miss them, but it's better than them winding up as old maids," the farmer shrugged.

9th Day of Christmas

On the ninth day of Christmas, my true love gave to me, nine ladies dancing.

The Tatton Park Ball was always a sight to see. The servants from all the houses in the neighbourhood were invited to their own dance on the same night as the great Tatton Park Ball. The dance began at the same time as the ball, though most of the servants from Tatton Park had to wait until after the grand dinner had been served before they could attend.

It was the responsibility of the most senior functionary in the neighbour to organise the servants dance, and for the last few years, that responsibility had fallen to Bosworth.

The butler from Grangeback had been honoured when he had first been handed the task after the butler for Duffleton Hall had retired, but he had soon discovered that it was something of a double-edged sword.

There was far more planning needed for the dance than Bosworth had first anticipated. The plans and timings from the Tatton Park Ball had to be taken into account to make sure that the servants that had to work would be able to eat with all their comrades.

The other difficulty was ensuring that there were people to drive the ladies and gentlemen home from the Tatton Park Ball, as well as the servants. The coachmen were often too drunk to stand, let alone drive, by 8 o'clock in the evening. So Bosworth paid farmers and their farmhands to man the carriages.

The question of who would prepare the food, how it would be served, who would provide the music and where the alcohol would come from were also the cause of no small amount of stress for the Grangeback butler.

Musicians were temperamental creatures that Bosworth tried to avoid at the best of times, and over Christmas, they were in demand.

Cooky was often tasked with preparing the food

and Bosworth went to Wilson at the inn in Stickleback Hollow for the alcohol.

The party was funded by all the houses in the neighbourhood. The families each put a set amount into a fund that Bosworth then had to spend on the party, but he did have to present receipts and an account book to show that the funds were not being misspent.

Most of the preparations had to be made months before the party to ensure that everything was prepared. It was normally late August when Bosworth called on each of the houses to collect the money, making a note in the record as to which households had paid, and how much they had given.

Though there was a set amount that each household was duty-bound to donate, most of the household tried to outdo their neighbours' generosity. The first year, Bosworth had greatly struggled to spend the sums he was given, so the remaining funds were donated to charities that were collecting in the neighbourhood.

When he had presented the account book to be

checked by the households, and the charitable donations had been discovered, the sums that were given to the party increased the next year.

A few weeks before the dance and the Tatton Park Ball, Miss Baker was extremely busy making repairs to dresses and new dresses for those that could afford the extravagance.

On Christmas Eve, the dresses were all collected, and there was an air of excitement that surrounded the village. The new maids at Grangeback had never been to a dance before and were all excited by the prospect of meeting young men in the service of other households. Those with partners looked forward to dancing into the early hours, whilst others looked forward to a night seeing old friends.

Gossip was often exchanged at the dance, but this was not something that Bosworth had to organise – gossip spread without any help from the butler.

The night of the dance and the ball, the farmers and the farmhands arrived at the different houses to drive the ladies and gentlemen to the Tatton Park Ball and the servants to the dance.

There was happy chatter from the servants, and as the carts and traps rolled along, they sang festive songs, wrapped up tightly in the cloaks and capes. At the dance, the beer flowed, and the music played.

The following day, each household was alive with talk of how well Bosworth had done with the dance, and how eagerly the servants awaited the next dance.

For weeks afterwards thank you notes arrived at Grangeback that were all addressed to Bosworth. Two of the maids had begun romantic entanglements that would certainly fuel some neighbourhood gossip for a few months to come.

All-in-all it was agreed that Bosworth should be in charge of organising all the dances in the future, but Bosworth thought that organising one dance a year was more than enough for him.

10th Day of Christmas

On the tenth day of Christmas, my true love gave to me, ten drummers drumming.

The sound of the regimental drums beat slowly in the stiffly Indian heat. It was a strange thing to pass Christmas in the heat of the Indian sun, but it was a welcome change to the cold winters that Brigadier Webb-Kneelingroach, Lieutenant Lewisham and Lieutenant Montgomery Baird were all used to.

The young lieutenants had been quite excited about their first posting to Asia, though the days of Assaye had passed and Napoleon was rotting on the island of St. Helena, there was still unrest in some parts of India.

All three men had been present at the battle of Waterloo – a battle that had made the names of many heroes and provided Sir Arthur Wellesley with an estate in Hampshire and a status that few could ever aspire to.

Things in India were very different to the battlefields of France. There were no formal balls that the lieutenants were invited to this year. There seemed to be something unpleasant brewing that had the men all on edge, but none of the lower-ranked officers had any inkling as to what that might be.

The drummers beat the slow tempo for the drills to be performed to. The brigadier came out of the officers' mess and stood watching the drills. When they had finished, the parade was called to attention in front of the brigadier.

He knew that the men were nervous about the rumours that were circulating; some of the more wild and outlandish than others, but there was nothing more certain to destroy morale than rumour.

"Men, I have a story to tell you. It is a story about a battle that was fought here not so long ago. Before I begin, take a drink and sit down. The tale is a long one, and I wouldn't want anyone fainting partway through."

The men all glanced at one another with confusion but did as the brigadier instructed. When the men had settled, the brigadier cleared his throat and began his story,

"The battle of Assaye was fought 14 years ago, and Sir Arthur Wellesley was in command of our forces. The Mahrattas had 30,000 horsemen, 12,000 infantry, 16 battalions that had been trained by and were led by French officers and 100 guns. Wellesley's forces were outnumbered, but despite this, the Duke of Wellington didn't hesitate to attack.

"He had four infantry regiments, seven infantry regiments, five Madra native regiments and some irregular cavalry from Mysore. His forces totalled 6,500 men and 22 guns."

Whispers ran around the assembled men. They all knew of the battle of Assaye, some had friends that had served at the battle, but none of the men there had. Only the brigadier had been there.

"The day was won, though men were lost, the men of the 74th Highlanders were the key to Sir Arthur Wellesley's victory. You may think of the men marching in kilts, but there wore white linen trousers. Only one officer from the regiment survived unscathed, the others were all either killed or wounded. They were ordered to march on the enemy guns. The 19th Light Dragoons saved the regiment from the charge of the Maratha cavalry. The advanced to the sound of pipes and drums, they marched steadily through the firing gun and captured two lines of enemy guns."

"There were many acts of bravery on that field, though the losses were high, the enemy were defeated with but a fraction of their numbers. It is the day that British blades triumphed over the guns of Daulat Scindia and the Raja of Berar. Though there were those that were ready to break and run, the line stood firm. At the battle of Waterloo, we sent Napoleon and his remaining forces packing.

"No matter what rumours you may hear, there is no need to lose heart. We are British, we stand against tyranny, we stand against insurmountable odds, and we emerge victorious," the brigadier shouted the last and the men cheered. Some leapt to their feet and thrust their guns in the air.

"I know that it is hard to be far from home and that thoughts of Christmas with your family will make it all the harder, but you are following in the footsteps of heroes and there is no greater honour than serving your country," the brigadier finished and dismissed the parade.

"What was the point in telling that story, sir?" Lieutenant Montgomery Baird asked as he and Lieutenant Lewisham followed the brigadier back to the officers' mess.

"Morale is as important to the army as much as anything else. Without high morale, the men won't fight. If the spirits of the men are too low, then we have lost before the enemy even comes into view. Sometimes it is important to remind them of the heroes that have fought before them and the great victories that have been won," the brigadier smiled.

11th Day of Christmas

On the eleventh day of Christmas, my true love gave to me, eleven pipers piping.

Being a Welshman in England was not always the easiest thing in the world. Constable Evans had spent most of his life listening to derogatory remarks about his homeland, his family and even himself.

In Stickleback Hollow, he rarely encountered any hostility, it wasn't like most other places in England, but in Chester, there was often some animosity.

Around Christmas, it was the worst though. He often missed his mother and father, but at Christmas, it was much worse than any other time of year. He missed spending Christmas Eve with his father listening to the pipes being played.

Though he wasn't Scottish, his family was musical, and there was nothing they appreciated more than listening to the pipes being played.

In the village he grew up in there had been a retired Highlander who would stand outside the church on Christmas Eve and pipe the congregation into the service.

Grace had listened to Arwyn telling stories about Christmas in Wales and noticed the hint of sadness that entered his voice and the pained expression that flittered across his face when he spoke about Christmas Eve.

She had tried in vain to find a piper that would come to Stickleback and pipe the congregation into the church. On the 11th day of Christmas, there was a market that saw a wide range of crafts and sweet treats from around the country being sold to celebrate the New Year.

It was an eclectic mix of items and people that Grace always visited. Lady Sarah had been whisked away to Duffleton Hall for the day but had given Grace permission to go as long as Constable Evans went with her.

The weather was dry, though there was a cold chill to the wind, but the market was busy with people marvelling at the trinkets and clamouring for treats to take home to their families.

Arwyn had been quite content to follow Grace around the market and watch as she bought perfumes for Lady Sarah and treats for Cooky and Mrs Bosworth. There was nothing that particularly appealed to the constable about the market, but it made a nice change to not be in Chester on duty.

It was nearing 2 o'clock when Grace decided that she wanted to visit the cathedral before they returned to Grangeback.

As the pair left the market, the sound of pipers playing drifted through the air to them. It grew louder the closer they got to the cathedral. Lining the path to the front of the cathedral stood eleven pipers.

Grace led Arwyn down the path, past the line of pipers, the constable's eyes tearing up as they went. As they reached the doors to the cathedral, Arwyn noticed that there were some familiar faces that stood just inside the doors.

Lady Sarah, Mr Hunter, Brigadier Webb-Kneelingroach, Lord Daniel Cooper, Thomas and

Edward Egerton, Doctor Hales, Miss Baker, Henry Cartwright and a host of other people from the neighbourhood were all waiting for him.

As he walked into the cathedral, the organ began playing. The sound of singing rose to meet him from the choir stalls. He blinked as he looked and saw his parents, his brothers, sisters and their families, all stood in the stalls, singing the same songs that they sang on Christmas Eve in Wales.

"But how?" Arwyn asked of nobody in particular.

"You looked so sad when you talked about Christmas in Wales and how long it had been since you saw your family. You've been so kind to me since I came to Grangeback and Stickleback Hollow that I wanted to do something nice for you," Grace explained.

"Thank you," Constable Evans choked before he slowly walked down to join his family and the singing. His friends filed out of the cathedral to let them enjoy their reunion privately.

"Thank you, George," Sarah said, turning to the Dean of Chester.

"You are most welcome. It's not quite the adventure that you brought the last time I saw you, but it is a very worthy cause," George Davys smiled at Sarah, "and like my beloved Marianne says, 'Christmas is a time for blessing our fellow men.'"

"It does seem fitting to do so, especially for a man that does so much for each of us," replied the brigadier.

12th Day of Christmas

On the twelfth day of Christmas, my true love gave to me, twelve lords a leaping, eleven pipers piping, ten drummers drumming, nine ladies dancing, eight maids a milking, seven swans a swimming, six geese a laying, five gold rings, four colly birds, three French hens, two turtle doves and a partridge in a pear tree.

Winchester was a quiet place at Christmas, except when the school had become snowed in. Though the farmers had tried to clear the roads, it had become an impossible task as the snow had fallen so quickly and the temperature had plummeted to the depths of cold that made the farmers unwilling to take their horses out of their warm stables.

The boys would have normally returned to their families for a few weeks over the festive period, but with the snow preventing the mass exodus, the boys were forced to stay in the school.

Mr Alexander Hunter did not enjoy his days at Winchester. The lessons seemed irrelevant to real life, and he was treated as an inferior by all the other boys that attended the school.

If it had been a school that the other young men from his neighbourhood had not attended, then there was a possibility that Mr Hunter would have enjoyed school life, but as it was, the moment he had arrived, he had been marked.

He had passed the exams with ease and proven that he was as scholastically capable as any of the other boys, but that hadn't mattered. He was an orphan and a bastard – two things that were unforgivable in the eyes of his schoolmates.

Mr Hunter had been looking forward to returning to Stickleback Hollow and spending his few weeks of respite with the groundskeeper, learning more about hunting and how to take care of a great estate like Grangeback.

Instead, he was walking the grounds of Winchester, trying desperately to avoid the other boys.

They didn't just subject him to psychological torment, but physical torment as well.

The last time they had cornered him, twelve of the boys had set upon him. Though they had beaten him black and blue, Mr Hunter had given as good as he got. One of the boys had broken his arm, and another had broken his nose.

The masters did nothing to curtail the violence in the school, as far as they were concerned, if they didn't see it, it wasn't happening.

The grounds provided Mr Hunter with some respite from the boys. Most of them preferred roaming the halls to the outdoors.

However, when it snowed, that wasn't always the case.

"HUNTER!" the sound of Mr Harry Taylor shouting caused Alex to turn. Across the lawn, he could see twelve boys advancing towards him. There was nowhere for Alex to hide, but there was plenty of space for him to run.

The young man set off at the fastest pace he could

in the snow. The powder sprayed up around his feet as he struggled to stay upright.

The twelve boys pursued him. Mr Harry Taylor, Mr Daniel Cooper, Mr Jake Walker, Mr Dominic Smith, Mr Thomas Egerton, Mr Edward Egerton, Mr Samuel Jones, Mr Stuart Moore, Mr Luke Broad, Mr Riki Ball, Mr Joe Blatherwick, and Mr Michael Hutton. Ten of the boys had been involved in the previous assault on Mr Hunter, Mr Timothy Wood and Mr Gregory Kitts were absent this time as they were both still being looked after by the Matron in the infirmary.

Mr Hunter made his way across the lawn towards the copse that lay to his right. The pack was gaining on him as they were following in his footsteps. Some tripped and fell into the fresh powder, but they were soon on their feet again.

As Alex reached the wood, the snow on the ground lessened, making it easier to run. In the trees, Mr Hunter had the advantage. He was far more at home in the woods than he was in corridors of Winchester.

The boys continued their pursuit into the trees.

There were small bushes and fallen trees that transformed their chase into an obstacle course. The twelve boys had to leap over all manner of undergrowth to try and keep pace with Mr Hunter.

As there was less snow on the ground, it became harder for the boys to keep track of where Alex had gone.

Mr Hunter trod as lightly as he could without losing speed, leaving few indications that he had passed through the trees. He managed to keep ahead of the chase and even caused the boys to lose sight of him.

When he was sure that he had left them far enough behind, Mr Hunter found a tree to climb. He clambered up as high as he could and then sat as still as possible.

Though there were no leaves on the trees, the branches provided some cover, as long as he stayed still. He was breathing heavily as he leaned against the trunk of a great oak and did his best not to pant.

"Damn it all. We've lost him," Mr Moore cursed. Mr Hunter could hear that they were nearby, but he daren't move to look.

"He can't have gone far," Mr Ball replied.

"There's no point trying to find him now. It'll be dark soon. He'll have to come back to the dorms. We can wait for him there. He needs to pay for the injuries he gave to Barmy and Sticks," Mr Hutton growled.

"We'll get him another day. It's not like he's going anywhere," Mr Broad sighed. The twelve boys were exhausted from the chase and had no intention of wasting time trying to find where Mr Hunter had gone.

Alex sat and listened to the sound of the boys leaving and resolved that when he was able to leave the school, he would, and he wouldn't be coming back.

Looking for more than just books? You can get the latest releases from me, signed paperbacks and hardbacks, mugs, t-shirts, journals and much more from my Read Round the Clock Shopify store.

~*~*~

Love the Mysteries of Stickleback Hollow? Not caught up with the rest of the series, then jump back to _A Thief in Stickleback Hollow_, Book 1 in the Mysteries of Stickleback Hollow and see how it all began.

The Mysteries of Stickleback Hollow: 12 Days of Christmas in Stickleback Hollow

About the Series
Mysteries abound

When her parents die from fever, Lady Sarah

Montgomery Baird Watson-Wentworth has to leave

India, a land she was born and raised in, and travel to

England for the first time. Finding it almost impossible to

adjust to London society, Sarah flees to the county of

Cheshire and the country estate of Grangeback that

borders the village of Stickleback Hollow. A place filled

with oddballs, eccentrics and more suspicious characters

than you can shake a stick at, Sarah feels more at home

in the sleepy little village than she ever did in the big

city, however, even sleepy little villages have mysteries

that must be solved.

Set in Victorian England, the Mysteries of Stickleback

Hollow follows the crime solving efforts of Constable

Arwyn Evans, Mr. Alexander Hunter and Lady Sarah Montgomery Baird Watson-Wentworth. From theft to murder, supernatural occurrences and missing people, Stickleback Hollow is a magical place filled with oddballs, outcasts, rogues, eccentrics and ragamuffins.

About the Author

I was born in Macclesfield, Cheshire, UK, and raised in the nearby town of Wilmslow. From an early age I discovered I had a flair and passion for writing.

I began writing at the age of 7 and was first published in 2010. I currently live with my partner, Matt, and our two cats in Christchurch, New Zealand.

As an avid horsewoman and gamer, I also have a passion for singing, dancing, the theatre, and my garden.

Facebook:

https://www.facebook.com/AuthorC.S.Woolley

Instagram: https://www.instagram.com/thecswoolley

Website: http://.mightierthanthesworduk.com

Acknowledgements

Writing can be an extremely lonely profession at times, but thankfully I never have to go through any of the pressures alone. My wonderful Matthew has been a source of constant support to me during all of my writing endeavours since we first met. I couldn't ask for a more fitting partner to share my life or love with.

Writing is not something I stumbled into either, my mother, Helen, took me, and my sisters, to the library every weekend when we were young to get different books, and I always maxed out the number of books I could get. Not only did she encourage me to read, but to write as well. To say I have been writing stories and poetry since I was 7 is not an exaggeration and the development of my writing career is due in no small part to her.

My mother-in-law, Lesley, has also been a source of

unflinching and unwavering support, something I could not do without.

To Laura and Sam, who have read and offered opinions, death threats and encouragement on my early drafts, you are true treasures. Amy, you too are worth your weight and more in gold for all your love and support.

It may seem that writers only function alone, but I am blessed to be part of an amazing community of authors whom I know that I have helped push me to even greater heights and success. So to Quinn Ward, Donna Higton, Scarlett Braden Moss, Bryan Cohen, Chez Churton, Robert Scanlon, Jen Lassalle, Brittany Weese, Phoebe Ravencroft, and Marcel Liemant, my dear friends, thank you.

And finally, to you, dear reader, without you there would be no books, no series, no career. I want to thank you for all the time that you spend reading my work, reviewing it, sharing it with your friends and family.

Without you there would be nothing. Thank you from the bottom of my heart.

Until we meet again in my next book, thank you and adieu.